P9-ECP-528

-Read Book

Who Feels Sad, Dear Dragon?

by Margaret Hillert
Illustrated by Jack Pullan

NORWOOD HOUSE 🏠 PRESS

DEAR CAREGIVER,

The *Beginning-to-Read* series is comprised of carefully written books that extend the collection of classic readers you may remember from your own childhood. Each book features text comprised of common sight words to provide your child ample practice reading the words that appear most frequently in written text. The many additional details in the pictures enhance the story and offer the opportunity for you to help your child expand oral language and develop comprehension.

Begin by reading the story to your child, followed by letting him or her read familiar words and soon your child will be able to read the story independently. At each step of the way, be sure to praise your reader's efforts to build his or her confidence as an independent reader. Discuss the pictures and encourage your child to make connections between the story and his or her own life. At the end of the story, you will find reading activities and a word list that will help your child practice and strengthen beginning reading skills.

Above all, the most important part of the reading experience is to have fun and enjoy it!

Shannon Cannon

Shannon Cannon, Ph.D., Literacy Consultant

Norwood House Press • P.O. Box 316598 • Chicago, Illinois 60631
For more information about Norwood House Press please visit our website at
www.norwoodhousepress.com or call 866-565-2900.
Text copyright ©2018 by Margaret Hillert. Illustrations and cover design copyright ©2018 by Norwood House Press, Inc. All rights reserved. No part of this book may be reproduced or utilized in any form or by any means without written permission from the publisher.

LIBRARY OF CONGRESS CATALOGING-IN-PUBLICATION DATA
  Names: Hillert, Margaret, author. | Pullan, Jack, illustrator.
  Title: Who feels sad, Dear Dragon? / by Margaret Hillert ; illustrated by
    Jack Pullan.
  Description: Chicago, IL : Norwood House Press, [2017] | Series: A
    beginning-to-read book | Summary: "A boy, with his pet dragon, feel sad
    after making bad behavior choices. The mood is brightened when the boy
    starts telling the truth, sharing, and making good choices. This title
    includes reading activities and a word list"-- Provided by publisher. |
    Identifiers: LCCN 2016052255 (print) | LCCN 2017014200 (ebook) | ISBN
    9781684040063 (eBook) | ISBN 9781599538235 (library edition : alk. paper)
  Subjects: | CYAC: Sadness--Fiction. | Behavior--Fiction. | Dragons--Fiction.
  Classification: LCC PZ7.H558 (ebook) | LCC PZ7.H558 Wgv 2017 (print) | DDC
    [E]--dc23
  LC record available at https://lccn.loc.gov/2016052255

Hardcover ISBN: 978-1-59953-823-5   Paperback ISBN: 978-1-68404-001-8

302N—072017
Manufactured in the United States of America in North Mankato, Minnesota.

No, no.
I want this toy.
I do not want to play with you.

I want that toy!
I want to play!

What is going on?
This is not good.

This is my car.
I do not want you to have it.

This is not a good choice.
You need time to think.

You sit here. And you sit there.

I am sad here.
I want to play.
I will do better.

Is think time over?

Yes, we are sad that we did that.
We will share when we play.

Mother, Mother!
I am home.

Come here!
Come here!
How was your day?

I was not good.
I did something.
It made me sad.

That was not a good choice.
You need to share at school.

Now, let me see.
Do you have homework?

No, I do not have homework.

Are you sure?
You need to tell me.

What is this?
You do have homework.

That was not a good choice.
You need time to think.

I am sad here.
I want Mother to be happy.
I will do better.

I am sorry.
I am sad I did that.
I will do my homework now.

Mother, Mother!
I am done with my homework.
Can I play now?

This is good!
Yes, you can play.
Have fun!

I will do better.
I will make good choices.
I will not be sad.
I will play now.
But first, I will do this.

Here you are with me.
And here I am with you.
Now it is a good day, Dear Dragon!

The following activities support the findings of the National Reading Panel that determined the most effective components for reading instruction are: Phonemic Awareness, Phonics, Vocabulary, Fluency, and Text Comprehension.

Phonemic Awareness: The /s/ sound

Oddity Task: Say the /**s**/ sound for your child. Say the following words aloud. Ask your child to say the word that does not end with the /**s**/ sound in the following word groups:

share, pass, class	kiss, hug, miss	this, his, her
more, lots, less	toss, throw, miss	toys, play, cars
sad, jokes, goes	pups, paws, think	

Phonics: The letter Ss

1. Demonstrate how to form the letters **S** and **s** for your child.

2. Have your child practice writing **S** and **s** at least three times each.

3. Ask your child to point to the words in the book that start with the letter **s**.

4. Write down the following words and ask your child to circle the letter **s** in each word:

sit	this	sad	is	share
was	something	yes	should	choices
school	first	see	sure	sorry

Vocabulary: Opposites

1. This story features the concepts of happy and sad. Discuss opposites and ask your child to name the opposites of the following:

   cool (warm)   good (bad)   dark (light)   big (little)

   boy (girl)   down (up)   go (stop)   loud (quiet)

2. Write each of the words on separate pieces of paper. Mix the words up and ask your child to put the opposite pairs back together.

Fluency: Shared Reading/CLOZE

1. Reread the story with your child at least two more times while your child tracks the print by running a finger under the words as they are read. Ask your child to read the words he or she knows with you.

2 Reread the story, stopping occasionally so your child can supply the next word. For example, Do you have_____ ? (homework), or I will make good _____ (choices), or I will _____ (play) now.

3. Now have your child reread the story, stopping occasionally for you to supply the next word.

Text Comprehension: Discussion Time

1. Ask your child to retell the sequence of events in the story.

2. To check comprehension, ask your child the following questions:

   • What were the two boys arguing about on page 6?

   • Why did the teacher tell the boys they needed time to think?

   • Why was Mother upset on page 20?

   • How did the boy feel when Mother sent him to think?

WORD LIST

Who Feels Sad, Dear Dragon? uses the 70 words listed below.

The **4** words bolded below serve as an introduction to new vocabulary, while the other 66 are pre-primer. You may wish to write the words on index cards and use them to help your child build automatic word recognition. Regular practice with these words will enhance your child's fluency in reading connected text.

a	day	happy	made	sad	want
am	dear	have	make	school	was
and	did	here	me	see	we
are	do	home	mother	share	what
at	done	**homework**	my	sit	when
	dragon	how		something	will
be			need	sorry	with
better	first	I	no	sure	
but	fun	is	not		
		it	now	tell	
can	going			that	yes
car	good	let	on	there	you
choice (s)			over	**think**	your
come				this	
			play	time	
				to	
				toy	

ABOUT THE AUTHOR
Margaret Hillert has helped millions of children all over the world learn to read independently. She was a first grade teacher for 34 years and during that time started writing books that her students could both gain confidence in reading and enjoy. She wrote well over 100 books for children just learning to read. As a child, she enjoyed writing poetry and continued her poetic writings as an adult for both children and adults.

Photograph by Glenna Washburn

ABOUT THE ILLUSTRATOR
A talented and creative illustrator, Jack Pullan, is a graduate of William Jewell College. He has also studied informally at Oxford University and the Kansas City Art Institute. He was mentored by the renowned watercolor artists, Jim Hamil and Bill Amend. Jack's work has graced the pages of many enjoyable children's books, various educational materials, cartoon strips, as well as many greeting cards. Jack currently resides in Kansas.